101 Eme~~rg~~ ~~~~ Don'ts:

A Guidebook for Patients and Visitors

emergency

<u>noun</u>, often attributive | emer·gen·cy | /əˈmərjənsē/

Definition of EMERGENCY
plural **emergencies**

an unforeseen combination of circumstances or the resulting state that calls for immediate action

Whether it's the neighborhood you grew up in, the circle of people you associate with, a job you've had, a place you've visited, a sports team, or club you've been a part of, it doesn't matter. I can guarantee you that no matter where you've been or what you've been a part of, it has had a guideline of unwritten rules to follow. You may not of been aware of them and you may have even violated some of the unwritten laws in your journey. This way of life applies to visits at any emergency department in any hospital in any country. Every time you walk into one there is a book of unwritten customs and courtesies, accompanied by an infinite amount of things you just don't do. The book of unwritten laws is too heavy to pick up and too long to read until the end. Just about every move you make can be detrimental to the way you're treated during your stay.

Emergency departments are overcrowded and short staffed all across the nation. This leads to absurd wait times, which collectively frustrates staff, patients, and visitors. In many situations tempers flare and patients or visitors begin to pester and verbally abuse the staff who have no control over the situation. People seem to lose their minds under these conditions, as physical violence is not above some patients and visitors. With over 10 years of experience in a Level-1 Trauma Center, I have both witnessed and experienced this on more occasions than I would like to remember. These outbursts can affect the staff's attitude towards your care and willingness to help make your long wait as pleasurable as possible. I have noticed a lot of patients and visitors seem to think the more they act out, the more help they will receive. This is absolutely false, and will do nothing more than perhaps increase your wait time and make your stay even a little less enjoyable than it already has been. Employees who work in emergency departments are very good at mastering how to have two personalities. Sure, we will talk to you with an extremely professional demeanor, but that demeanor completely changes once we get back to conversing with coworkers. We are going to talk about how annoying, weak, or ignorant the person is we were just dealing with.

There is a lot that can happen during your stay in the ED. You can bet that it will be overcrowded with a plethora of personalities mashed together during extremely long wait times. A lot can go wrong with such a cocktail for disaster. There are a lot of things you can do to make your stay as pleasant as possible and maintain the respect of staff members.

You might be wondering how you can help yourself as a patient or visitor in the emergency department. After all, you're not in the medical field, and being in an emergency department can be overwhelming if you're not used to it. It would seem with overcrowding, long wait times, countless wrong moves you can make, combined with a staff with busted morale, that you just can't win being on the other side. Have no worries, I'm here to help guide you through your stay in the department with all of the experience I have gained over the years. If you follow these *101* rules I have torn from the pages of the unwritten emergency department rule book, staff will be more than willing to help you with a smile on their face. Most importantly, you'll be close to being the perfect patient or visitor, and you won't be labeled a whiny bitch or an ignorant dick. You did not see that coming, did you? Oh yeah, we curse like sailors and have one hell of a sick sense of humor. Study the fuck out of these rules before you have an emergency and you will be just fine. Choose not to study and you'll find yourself in a world of hell during your stay. The next *101 Don'ts* will touch base on just about every step through the process of your stay. I am showing you the water. All you have to do is drink for a pleasurable experience.

Let us begin with just simply entering the building and starting the sign-in process. There is quite a bit you can fuck up on in these first few crucial moments...

1) **Don't enter the department with a sack of food or coffee.**

   If you walk in that door with a bag of food from your favorite fast food restaurant, or a coffee from your favorite coffee shop you better be a fucking visitor! You have already lost all credibility as a patient before you even begin to sign in if it is for yourself. What part of emergency do you not understand? You mean to tell me you had to rush to the hospital, but you had time to stop and get some food or something to drink first? Come on, do really expect anyone to take you seriously? You might as well take your ass right back outside, get in your car, and go enjoy that shit in the comfort of your own home because you are not going to be seen by a doctor any time soon. If you're that hungry or thirsty, at least have the common decency to finish it before you walk in that entrance. Having an emergency, but stopping at McDonald's on your way in just doesn't add up motherfucker. Chances are you're not getting anything you came looking for, including respect and sympathy. The only acceptable time you can pull this move is if you got shot or stabbed at the place you were buying it. Then it's cool, we'll understand why you carried your food and drink inside the emergency department.

2) **Don't sign in with multiple complaints.**

   Unless you just got hit by a car, fell off a building, or some other shit that would damage your entire body, you cannot complain about head to toe problems. If you say some off the wall stuff like you have a headache, your stomach hurts, and you sprained your ankle last week, the nurse signing you in blacked out a long time ago and most likely just wrote down "multiple complaints". This is not a place to get a full physical because you have nothing better to do with your time. You get one complaint, so choose it wisely. You know, unless they are tied together. Something like you are lightheaded because you lost so much blood from the wound you would like to stitched up, then we'll add that complaint.

3) **Don't sign in for a fever without taking anything for a fever.**

So, you have a fever and you came to the emergency department before you took any over the counter fever medications. Guess what you're about to receive? Some over the fucking counter medications! Fucking think. You probably even had some fucking Tylenol or Motrin at home. It's like fucking magic, you swallow a couple of pills and your fever disappears. Now if you have been popping those like candy for the past few days and it's not working, by all means come to the ED. If you are here before you tried any fever reducers at home, get the fuck home and try some, and quit wasting my fucking time. You probably could have scored some from the place you picked your combo meal up from and killed your fever and hunger at a one-stop shop.

4) Don't say your pain is greater than 10.

Dickhead, I just told you on a scale of 1 to fucking 10. Not 15, 20, "way worse than 10", "your scale doesn't go high enough", I said 10 motherfucker. Don't try to act like you're some kind of superhero standing in front of me, because your pain shatters the pain scale. In my personal opinion, a 10, is comparable to just winning a wrestling match against two alpha lions over a steak. Looking at you, I can see you're somewhere between 1 and 1.5 on the pain level. Don't bullshit me. I'll put a 10 down but nobody is going to believe your bitch ass. Chances are everyone on the clock is working through more pain than what you're experiencing. Be honest or be judged. At least impress me with a cool story as to why it is just so severe.

5) Don't have someone else speak for you while you're signing in.

Unless you're so young you haven't learned how to speak yet, this is unacceptable. Well, I guess that's a lie as there are some circumstances that will make this acceptable. You can have someone speak for you if you're holding your vocal cords together with your hands. Other than that, grow the fuck up and tell me why you are here because I am not writing shit until you speak up. Seriously, unless your physically unable to speak or there is a language barrier, muster up enough strength to get a few sentences out and save some pride.

6) **Don't ask if the person that wants to sign in has to come inside.**

No, no, just have them wait in the car. I totally trust a person I've never met before will give me accurate personal data and reason for wanting to be seen by a doctor. We'll just have you go get them when we're ready for them. YES! Yes, they have to come the fuck in. We need a visual of them and to hear what they have to say about what brings them to the emergency department. We will not sign them in until they come in the building. Jesus Christ. You think you can just come in and tell me what's wrong with your friend and I'll give you a couple pills and prescriptions for the road? Get the patient the fuck in here, or get the fuck out of here.

7) **Don't arrive via ambulance for some weak shit.**

Yeah, a lot of you motherfuckers don't know this one. A lot of the ambulances driving up and down your highways are transporting shit like toothaches and earaches. Yup, some punk bitches are calling 911 for shit like that. If you think because you arrive via ambulance you'll be seen quicker you're hysterically wrong. You're about to unstrap yourself from that ambulance stretcher and walk your ass to the waiting room. There you will wait with the other 60 people that signed in for bullshit emergencies. This is a really good way to get staff immediately pissed at you. That ambulance could be used for some other person truly in need and here you are fucking it up for them because you thought you would just call 911 for some weak ass bullshit. Use 911 like a drunk social media post. Think multiple times before you mash the buttons on that phone and make your shit public.

8) Don't lie to staff about your emergency.

I'm not really sure why patients think they can get away with this. It's almost like they think because we wear scrubs we're extremely naïve. In reality, emergency staff are really talented at sorting out bullshit and lies. There is also a tracking system that shows your visits and prescriptions you've recently had filled. We know your lying and would much rather have you shoot us straight, you'll get more respect that way. If you're looking for narcotics or a place to sleep inside from harsh weather, be honest. This way staff won't be all pissed off at you for all the bullshit orders they have to perform on your lying ass. Honesty will save both the patient and staff a lot of hassle and time. It will also help you get the proper care and resources you actually need. Emergency departments have all kinds of information on drug programs and homeless shelters. They'll even help you get there. So don't fucking lie to me and make me do a bunch of work I don't want to fucking do on you.

9) Don't come every fucking day.

This is when you get labeled a "frequent flyer". We already know your name, date of birth, and sometimes even your address. Guess what else we know? That you are full of shit, annoying as fuck, and that we have absolutely no intention of doing anything for you. All you are doing by frequenting the emergency department is pissing off staff and taking up a fucking seat in the waiting room. You can complain and ask how much longer it will be all you want. You can play like it's your first time there, but both you and I know what's up. Chances are you've pulled more shifts in there than some of the staff. If you want to play games we can play all fucking night, because I have more games than Milton Bradley and Parker Brothers on production day. No, you can't have a fucking turkey sandwich and ginger ale. You're lucky I'm giving you these saltines and water. Now get your annoying ass to the waiting room and don't ask me another fucking question until you hear your name called.

10) Don't lie about being a family member.

This is mainly for when a violent trauma comes in. Somebody gets shot, stabbed, or beat unconscious. So let me get this right, you are the victim's cousin or sibling but you only know their first name or what they go by on the streets? Shut the fuck up! I have family from coast to coast, some I have not seen in years. I know every one of their first and last names.

If I haven't seen them in such a long time that I forgot their real name or last name I'm damn sure not traveling to the hospital to visit them. How fucking stupid do you think staff is? You are not getting buzzed through the door and you can take your ass right back out of the exit. You will get absolutely nowhere with just a first name or a street name. If you don't know a person's name then you have no business being in the emergency department trying to visit them.

11) **Don't say your symptoms have been going on for years.**

Hold on. Hold on. Wait a minute, wait just a goddamn minute. You mean to tell me your back or stomach or whatever the fuck it was you just said has been bothering you for two fucking years, and you chose to come in this Monday morning at 0300? Oh no, please proceed, I want to hear all about why this is the morning you can't walk and are in that wheelchair. I'm sure the story I'm about to receive is truly heartbreaking, extremely complicated, and very fucking pitiful. Save your breath, because honestly I don't have the time nor the inclination to hear your long winded bullshit, and I'm sure the moral of the story will be that Dilaudid really helped the last time. I can only imagine how painful and sad the journey over the past few years that brought you here this morning really is. It would be nice to hear it all, it really would be, but here's your wristband. Now get

your ass out of that wheelchair and walk to the
waiting room until we call your name in a few hours.

12) Don't say your symptoms have been going on for fifteen minutes.

What the fuck are you even talking about? Let's first
discuss where you live and came from. Fifteen
minutes? That is a really impressive time to feel pain,
call 911, manage to throw on some pajama pants,
and catch a ride on an ambulance to my emergency
department. I'm more interested in being your sports
agent, and signing you a track and field contract for
the fucking US Olympic Team, than I am in signing
you in as a patient. Oh damn, I see you're already on
your phone with an agent and taking selfies. Here's
your wristband, now unstrap yourself from that
stretcher and walk your fifteen minute, tooth pain ass
to the waiting room. One of our caring staff members
will be calling you sometime between now and the
end of my shift. If they don't call you before my
twelve hour shift ends it's just as well, they'll
probably catch you on the next shift.

13) Don't say you have a doctor's appointment tomorrow.

You do realize you're going to be here until
tomorrow, correct? The wait is pushing double digit
hours and you want to sign in for the same exact
reason you have an appointment scheduled for
tomorrow morning. I'll sign you the fuck in, but

what I would really like to do is give you a life talk. Go home. Try to get some rest in the comfort of your own surroundings. Wake up in the morning and go see your doctor at your appointment. Chances are if you stay here you'll see a doctor around the same time as you already have scheduled to see one. It is not worth the added stress of being in the middle of the emergency department. Just turn around and leave. Go wait it out some place else.

14) Don't make it a family affair.

Ok, so I see you have three kids all with similar symptoms, understandable. None of the complaints are emergencies, but I can respect your concern. Oh, what's that, you're not done yet? Sure, we can get you seen as well, Mom. We'll get that problem you've been dealing with for weeks all fixed up while you're here. We're still not done signing in yet, are we? Get the fuck up here, Dad, I see it in your eyes that you need some help as well. Fuck it, what's your information? Let's bang this family physical out in the emergency department at 2300 on a school and work night. For fuck's sake it's a goddamn emergency department, not a family health center.

15) Don't bring your entire family or circle of friends.

You may be thinking, "Wait you just said that one, moron". On the contrary, you ignorant fuck, signing your entire family in is different from bringing your entire family while you are the only one that actually needs to be seen by a medical doctor. I have to be forward with you on this one, as soon as we see you walk in with your gaggle of emotional supporters, this screams to medical professionals that you and your entire crew are going to be nothing more than a gigantic cluster-fuck of dramatic bitches. By bitches, I don't mean Susan whose soy latte has too much foam on top. I'm talking about the weak-hearted dramatic bitches who think every little thing means you're dying and come up to bother staff every two minutes for an update. And you, the patient, the biggest bitch of them all, playing right in to this, soaking up all the attention you're getting from acting like a fool. These shenanigans do not motivate staff to help you out. In actuality what's going to happen is they will do the absolute bare minimum for you before you get to a room. After they medicate you with basic triage protocols and make you the subject of harsh jokes on break, they're going to play a game to see if you cry yourself to sleep or keep it up until you get that room. This is when one of three scenarios will play out. You'll either cry yourself to sleep and your crew will quit being pests until we finally get you back, you'll scream while your crew comes up every minute, or you'll get so pissed that staff isn't buying it that you'll leave. Either scenario, staff doesn't give a fuck. They blocked out your nonsense as soon as you started it and you leaving just opens up a spot in line at a place you didn't need to be to begin with. So let's just save everyone some time and sanity and not do that bullshit.

16) Don't act like you don't know what to do immediately after signing in.

This mainly applies to frequent flyers, but goes for you first timers as well. You just signed in, probably received your wristband and were given instructions on how to proceed. You're probably thinking this is unfair since signing into an emergency department usually occurs when a person is under some stress. Staff should have patience with the patients and visitors if they don't absorb all of the information they were just given. Well I'm going to tell you, that you are wrong. This defense would be understandable if it was some crazy instructions you were just given. It's not. We are talking about simply knowing your left from your right, sitting or standing, or a choice between which door to enter. It's preschool shit. I'll give you the benefit of the doubt that your mind was on something else and you weren't fully paying attention. Then I'm going to take that right back as there are literally signs everywhere. Take a look around at your surroundings and read a sign. If that fails you then do the thumb and index finger test. If it makes an "L" that's your left. Pay attention and read a fucking sign from time to time.

17) Don't say you wouldn't be here if you didn't have to be.

This is a classic emergency department line used by patients, who in fact, do not need to be there. A quick glance at your appearance paired with a quick listen to your complaint says we already started this visit based on a lie. Once this line is whipped out, you begin to build your story up, telling a tale that would amaze your average person, pushing them to believe you came here in a last resort effort. Save your breath. You're talking to a professional who most likely stopped paying attention to your bullshit story as soon as you used that line. They already feel you don't have to be there and chances are they recognize you from the last time you "wouldn't be here if you didn't have to be".

18) Don't say you have a high pain tolerance.

Well, to start, this is unnecessary information that anyone working in the ED could give a shit about. Once we get past that truth bomb let's talk about how you are clearly demonstrating you have what most ED staff would call a below average tolerance for pain. This always comes from the patient who has nothing deformed, bleeding, nor missing. This makes you look terrible, as staff watches you whine and flop around handling your pain at a below average tolerance trying to project on everyone just how high your tolerance actually is. That's a bad sales pitch, staff is not buying your bullshit, nor are they entertained by the fact that you're just trying to avoid the inevitable. Hey boss, save everyone some time, take your ibuprofen and have a seat in the waiting room with the fifty other people that have a high pain tolerance.

19) Don't go directly to the vending machine after you sign in.

I must say it's absurd that I even have to address this unwritten rule. Unfortunately, with my experiences, I do. Seriously? You just lost all hallway cred in the ED with that move. No staff is going to show respect for your story or complaint if you go buy a fucking soda and some chips after you get your wristband. This is where you just signed in for a medical emergency and your biggest concern is what snacks they have to offer? I can assure you there are several patients who see absolutely nothing wrong with this. I really am not sure how else I can word it so that you are able grasp just how fucking ridiculous this looks. I don't have the statistics in front of me right now, so I am unable to produce exact percentages for this next generalization about the vending machine situation. It has to be the 77-82% range that this behavior leads to complaining about lost money, or how it gave you the wrong product. Cool story, staff doesn't give a fuck. As a matter of fact, sit all that shit down, shut up and quit bitching. Frankly, staff wants to throw away that picnic you just bought, and cannot wait to embarrass you for having it to begin with. They are about to break down endless reasons you can't find on the internet, product by product, professionally humiliating and scolding you. Just save yourself the embarrassment, because it's one of the perks staff loves to pounce on. It's just going to end with you sitting back in the waiting room, next to the very vending machines from which you came, sipping on your carbonated beverage, eating soggy chips from all of your tears of shame dripping in the bag.

20) **Don't go directly to the bathroom after signing in.** This can really fuck up the flow and force staff to look at your pitiful face for a few extra, unnecessary hours. Now you're just going to have to use your own discretion on this one. This obviously does not apply to every patient and is going to vary from case to case. Since guidelines aren't strictly defined and common sense gets less common by the day in the ED, I'll break it down the best I know how and give you a loose reference point for bathroom courtesy. If you are pissing bloody, clotty, oddly tinted, foul smelling piss, they need a sample. If you are pissing a lot, or nothing at all, they will need a sample. What staff doesn't need a sample of, and will promptly advise you to throw in the trash, is a home packaged sample of your vomit or diarrhea. These samples are usually presented as gifts in small waste baskets, pots, big kitchen bowls, storage bags, or your common plastic grocery bag. Speaking of diarrhea,

unless you have it, don't immediately go take a shit. If it's a coin toss between dropping a load and signing in the ED that's weighing heavily on your mind, chances are you could have done that in the comfort of your own home before bringing us to this halt in progress.

See? You can really fuck up before your stay has even really started. Now that we got that out of the way, let me give you some tips while getting your blood pressure checked…

21) Don't ask if you have to take your arm out of your coat for a blood pressure.

Yes, yes you do. No, staff cannot obtain a pressure through your winter coat, sweater, long sleeve shirt, and thermal underwear. Take it the fuck off and save us both from blankly staring at each other. As long as you can stare with your highly protected arm extended out, ED staff can stare right back until you do what they need. Don't make a half-assed attempt at pulling it up a little either, just take your arm out. Being stubborn with this action is only going to play out one of three ways: You'll get a ridiculously inaccurate, made up, or undocumented blood pressure. Either way you're going right back to the waiting room. Might as well save both sides some frustration, take your arm out of your coat for literally two minutes, and get the first phase of the wait over with.

22) Don't say your blood pressure was high at the machine in the store.

Those things are as inaccurate as weathermen. It might be high, it might be low, it's like a slot machine every time you use it. You never know what combo it's about to land on. I'll leave you a no bullshit quote I heard a cardiologist once say about them. "I paid for both my kids' college education because of those machines." If that doesn't tell you how inaccurate they read, I'm not sure what will. Plus, I don't give a shit what it said, we go by the pressure in which I am about to document. Nobody cares about your drug store blood pressure.

23) Don't move around while getting your blood pressure checked.

This only makes your numbers less accurate, and chances are the cuff had to get extremely tight after several attempts of getting a reading. If need be, staff will hold your hand like a small child to keep you still. On the flip side, they'll also let you flop around and make that cuff get so tight it leaves bruises or explodes off of your arm, whichever comes first. I'm just really unsure of how to explain how childish this is. It is not a painful experience and can be over with in less than a minute if you just stay still. Quit trying to avoid the inevitable, take your ibuprofen, and head to the waiting room.

24) Don't tell me the blood pressure cuff is too tight.

Chances are this is your fault because of your personal lack of discipline and ability to stay still. If it's not from flopping, chances are it's still your fault because you have high blood pressure and fail to care for it properly. You shouldn't expect not to sweat when you're next to fire, just like you shouldn't expect your cuff not to get excessively tight when you know your pressure is high. It gets like that every time it's checked, yet you act like it's unbearable, and it's the first time you've encountered such a grip on your oversized arm. Yes, that pressure is high. Yes, that cuff just pinched and bruised you. No, staff doesn't care. No, it's not emergent. No, nobody cares how uncomfortable that made you. Yes, you may have a seat in the waiting room with everyone else who bitched about how tight their cuff got and how high their pressure was.

25) Don't say the blood pressure cuff is not the correct size.

This applies almost 99% of the time when both the patient and the staff member know damn right well it's the wrong sized cuff. You know it, I know it, everybody knows it. Let's just both pretend all is well, we'll get these bullshit numbers, and not strike up that awkward conversation. Of course the staff member trying drastic measures to make the adult large cuff fit on your wrist knows it's the wrong size. Just like they know they should have a neonatal cuff around your absent bicep, but they try their best. Let's be honest with each other, you haven't had an honest blood pressure since your kindergarten physical. Just go with it. Just take the outrageously inaccurate numbers with you to the waiting room like you always have in the past. No need to search the entire department for that one cuff we used ten years ago for the exact same type of patient that refused to accept their blood pressure. They too left with an inaccurate pressure, and discharge instructions to follow up some place else.

26) Don't say a normal blood pressure is really high or low for you.

Cool story, but I don't give a shit. Judging by every text book I've read and every person I've interacted with in the profession I'd say it's still not an emergent pressure and you just wasted both of our time. Look, you came here for help don't start telling me what is good and bad. You look fine and your pressure is right between the numbers it should be. Take that information with you to the waiting room and ponder over whether you really even need to be here.

Continuing with the vital signs process, let us dive a little deeper and discuss a couple other fuck-ups you can pull while this is happening…

27) Don't stick your middle finger out for a pulse ox to be applied.

This is a sign of disrespect, and the smirk on your face makes it quite evident it was intentional. So, you think you can flip the bird in a childish manner and smile about it, and everything is fine? Wrong. You're about to get disrespected on levels you can't comprehend and keep up with. Fuck me, huh? No, fuck you. That staff member no longer gives a shit about your complaints. They just can't wait to verbally fuck you with tearing apart your story and making you feel bad for even coming. That's like ordering a meal and flipping off the waiter as he takes it back to the cook. Dangerous. You immediately just fucked up your order. Extending that middle finger just earned you an ibuprofen the nurse blew on after dropping it on the floor. Your service level just plummeted and while you got a quick laugh and a little smirk out of giving that staff member the finger. They just went to everybody they know and told them of your childish ways. From now on every staff member will try their best to professionally extend a much longer middle finger.

28) Don't say equipment is being placed on you incorrectly.

No. No, it's really not, asshole. Guess what? These motherfuckers putting it on have gone through tremendous amounts of schooling and hands on training to make sure they are doing it correctly. You will not meet one ED staff member who doesn't pride themselves in what they're doing. They know what's up and they know how to execute their craft properly. When you try to inform them they are doing it all wrong they get defensive and super passive-aggressive. You're not going to get your way and even if it was completely wrong they will fake their way through it with complete confidence to make it work before they admit you were right. I mean why a patient would even say that unless they have some kind of special care kind of baffles me. Oh, you know how to use all this shit better than we do? Next time just drive up to the front doors and we'll have a runner bring you out a bag of supplies so you can just take it all home and care for yourself. After all, with all your knowledge and ability to do it better, it would save us both time, and you wouldn't have to come pose as a patient to teach medical professionals for free.

Unfortunately vitals take a few seconds to document. Here is some shit not to do during those few seconds…

29) Don't say you googled your symptoms.

Oh shit, I had no idea you took the time and effort to do extensive research before arrival. ED staff really appreciates when you do this. It makes them feel great that you just cancelled out years of education and experience with a ten minute internet search. Now that everyone knows you googled your symptoms and you know exactly how to handle this emergency we can skip all these bullshit tests and save some time. Fuck the half century worth of education the handful of people have that talked to you so far. We'll forget all the extra initials earned, years dedicated to education, and unmatchable hands on experience. This patient just googled their symptoms! Holy shit. Let's just give them a login to the computer so they can type up their own discharge instructions and prescriptions. We all know that's all you need anyway. You wouldn't even be here if you could do this shit from your home computer. Dumbass emergency department about to take ten hours to do what your google degree enables you to achieve in ten minutes.

30) Don't blow in a staff member's face.

You know what I'm talking about. That forceful exhale looking for sympathy, that's designed to express just how bad your pain is, aimed directly at the medical professional's nostril and mouth area. This face blow never comes from someone who just brushed their teeth and got done using mouthwash with a tantalizing flavored gum in their mouth. Nope. It comes from that person who hasn't brushed their teeth since yesterday morning. Since then they must have dined on a strict diet of dead skunk assholes with a bowl of shit stew. And if it's not coming from that type of motherfucker, it's coming from some rookie fueled up on liquor they bought in plastic bottles and puked at least a dozen times by the time that exhaled breath overtakes your senses and leaves you feeling angry and violated. Once again, I don't have the exact numbers from the extensive research done on the "blow vs blow" opinion amongst healthcare professionals. With an experienced guess, I'd have to say the percentages lie right around 70/30. "Blow vs blow", you ask? Yes. That means surveys conducted around the country in emergency departments found that roughly 70% of staff would rather get punched in the face by Mike Tyson while introducing themselves to patients and family. This is in comparison to the other 30% who would rather take your vomit and shit scented breath to the face. The odds clearly translate that you just don't fucking blow in the face of a professional.

31) **Don't cough without covering your mouth.**
The age on your chart indicates you are an adult of legal age, however, your actions say this is a lie. Nobody wants a sick person coughing and hacking all over them, and this holds true for healthcare professionals as well. This isn't preschool, you

should know this shit by now. And if you are in preschool, it's no excuse, work on covering your fucking mouth when you cough kid. Either way cover your mouth. It's disrespectful and disgusting. Work on your manners. It takes minimal effort to block your own cough, so there is really no excuse for any age group.

32) Don't be a moaner.

Why are you doing that? Are you having an orgasm, experiencing pain, or both? Staff can't call it, but they're taking bets on it. This is the ED, I think the porn auditions are being held in the next building over. Seriously, do you have a broken arm, or is your asshole being torn apart like tissue paper by a massive dick right now? Nobody knows, and the moaner never gives information. They moan nonstop for hours as if participating in breaking the record for the world's longest gangbang on a stretcher. All this does is make the staff laugh and mock you, annoy surrounding patients, and cause you to get hit on by a few hallway drunks. If that's your thing, then by all means proceed with the porno moan, just know it is not making staff think your complaint is any more serious than they already thought. They basically just waited by your side to see if you were actually masturbating or just acting. Either way they know those moans are not from an illness nor injury.

For you fake motherfuckers…

33) Don't fake a fall.

This is a very fast and efficient way to lose all respect from and anger staff. First off, in case you didn't know, most emergency departments have more cameras for surveillance than London. When a patient hits the ED floor, it creates endless amounts of forms and documentation to be completed. Of course they're going to check cameras to see whether your fall is legit or questionable, it saves their asses. Nurses and managers are crammed in the control room watching your tape, breaking it down frame by frame. They're watching it in slow motion, rewinding it over and over, breaking it down with more angles and expertise than sports analysts. That whole time you're thinking you just fooled everyone, they're in the replay booth laughing at your punk ass. Did you really think you could say you fell and everyone would just take your word for it? Well, if you did, I'm here to tell you that you're fucking wrong. Unless you like people breaking down just how fake you are, frame by frame, just save yourself the embarrassment of being confronted with facts about how fake you are.

34) Don't fake a seizure.

It's not a movie set, this is real life. Those aren't actors standing around watching your audition, they are trained medical professionals. You didn't just win an Emmy for best dramatic performance in a daytime soap opera, you just won worst performance in an emergency department. Not only is the staff unimpressed with your portrayal of a real seizure, they're pissed they wasted their time to come watch the show. That's all it is, a show. Sure you're going to get the attention of surrounding patients and staff. Sure everyone is going to worry and think there must be something really wrong with you. Then staff is going to give you a hundred reasons on why that was indeed fake. They aren't going to whisper them in your ear to save you some embarrassment either. No way. Staff is going to ridicule you and call you out on your mistakes, loudly. They want everyone to know why they're treating your seizure this way. They want other patients and visitors to see the shit staff deals with on a daily basis, and why their wait times are longer than necessary. And most importantly, they want you to know just how bad of an actor you are and that they will not be buying into your bullshit.

For the non-emergency department employees, don't be a d-bag…

35) Don't wear your wear your work badge if you're not working.

ED staff always finds this to be hilarious. While the employee, who is either a visitor or patient, thinks it holds weight, ED staff sees it as a fucking joke. The sad part is these blind fucks fail to realize why their badge from another unit gets no respect. You see, emergency staff is like the special forces of the medical community. They see everything first, execute a plan to control any situation, and do so with very little resources. From time to time they call in for help from other units to decompress the heat they have breathing down their necks. They took this job knowing it wouldn't be easy, and aren't surprised when help doesn't come the majority of time. They make calls and usually receive a big "fuck you" from the other end of the line. They're used to it so they don't dwell on it for long and make do with the situation they're in. Now hearing all that, why would you do that? Some fuck is flaunting a badge around that represents a unit who directly screws the ED on a daily basis, and is looking for special treatment. I'm not the smartest guy around, but even I can see that will get you nowhere. They take care of their own, who take care of them. It's a tight knit community and if you were one of them you wouldn't need your badge because they would recognize their own. Take yourself and your foreign badge to the waiting room with the rest of the population who don't work in the ED. Really? It's like saying, "yeah I fuck you over all the time, but we work in the same building so I deserve special treatment". Ha! If you don't work in this unit, you get shit treatment like all the other d-bags who think they're special.

This next one is strictly for the dudes…

36) Don't let your girlfriend or wife rub your head.
This is strictly a *Don't* for male patients. Look I'm all about being in touch with your feelings or whatever, and I understand that every man isn't built to be a "man's man". However, I'm also all about showing some pride, and understand a great majority of nurses are females. I also know for a fact that 100% of those female nurses are going back to their female peers to talk about how much of a bitch you are being. If you're cool with that, well then, I guess I am too. I just want to put it out there that you are not missing a Tuesday of 2nd grade, home with your mommy, watching cartoons, laying on the couch while she feeds you soup and rubs your head. You are in an emergency department, filled with females who are probably sicker than you, calling you a punk bitch and trying to take you seriously. Head rubs do feel incredible, but this is not the place, nor time.

Over the next several *Don'ts*, we'll cover questions you shouldn't ask and things you shouldn't say. These give away so many clues to how legit your complaint and visit are, shows so much about your character, as well as how often you frequent this establishment…

37) Don't ask which doctors are working during your visit.

Why? Are you neighbors, friends, old chums from childhood, or just know them all from being here way too fucking much? Chances are it is going to be the latter when this question is asked. ED staff immediately realizes you asked this because you have literally been cared for by every employee in this department. You are probably here for specific things, and asking this to get a feel of how your visit is going to play out. Yup, just like any profession there are weak links in the ED as well. You have experienced and studied every emergency physician's demeanor and tendencies. You know exactly how your treatment is going be laid out depending on which doctors are working. As soon as you asked that question, both you and staff know, it was merely a cover for what you really want to ask. Which is, should I stay or should I go? Staff wants to save time just as much as you do. That being said, if that is ever a question, you should go. Everyone will try to expose the weak link and try to prevent you from what you really want by working the system.

38) Don't ask how many doctors are working.

One. We have one fucking doctor seeing all 200 hundred patients here tonight. The ED really apologizes for the inconvenience. They called other doctors, but some were golfing or at a book club meeting, while others just didn't feel like coming in because of symptoms similar to your bullshit complaint. At a young age I learned there is no such thing as a stupid question. As an adult, I learned this was a lie, and how many doctors are working is one of them. It's not a lack of doctors that is causing your wait time to be so long, it's a plethora of weak bodies like yourself that causes the wait to be so long. There could be a 1:1 ratio of doctors to patients and it wouldn't be enough to satisfy the masses. Be assured that there is more than just one doctor dealing with all the bullshit emergencies the community decided to deem emergent on this busy evening. Just take your number and wait your turn or go home, either way I'm good with it.

39) Don't ask what area you are going to.

This is not meant to deter you from asking where you are going in the department, because you truly are curious and want to know your plan of care. You should absolutely ask in that case, and deserve an explanation. This is aimed at the fucks that ask because they already know how their plan of care is going to play out because of the area they are heading to. They know the layout of the department better than the employee they are asking. Once they have this information they can actually take over the route to the destination. The employee can just follow along while given a brief history lesson on every room they pass. Might as well throw on a sports jacket after your discharge and be a fucking tour guide in the lobby. Pick up some extra cash earning tips to pay for your ride home. Once again, if you are nervous and want information ask away. This is for the people who could build a model of the emergency department to scale with every intricate detail because they've been there so many goddamn times. You know who you are, staff knows who you are, and everybody knows you're an expert on the department. Just keep your mouth shut and quit bragging about how well you know the area without ever punching in to pull a shift. Nobody gives a shit about how many times you have been to a certain area or that you can give a history on each room built in the ED. Just shut your mouth and follow the staff member.

40) Don't ask why you are going to a room.

I'm not sure what worries me more about this question. The fact that you really don't know why, or that you ask it with sincerity. Chances are by the time you get a chance to ask this, you have probably been waiting at least 8-10 hours. You have complained about the wait, listened to others complain, took in all the intoxicating fragrances of bodily fluids and individuals who have not showered in who knows how long. You have sat in uncomfortable chairs or laid on an uncomfortable stretcher for hours on hours. This is the moment we've both been waiting for to arrive. The very reason you came! Now that we're here you want to ask why we are going? To see a fucking doctor, moron. Why else would you go to a room in the emergency department? You don't sign in and then staff just calls you back to sign your discharge papers after they feel you've spent enough hours in the waiting room watching television with the general population. I mean if you're not shy, staff isn't shy. I guess you can just drop your clothes for an assessment in the waiting room. If that's not your style, then quit asking dumb questions, and follow me to your fucking room.

41) **Don't ask if it is short staffed.**
Of course it's short staffed. Take a look around, motherfucker. There is literally standing room only, because stretchers are lining the halls filled with patients, not one seat left in the waiting room, and chaos in every direction you look. You don't need a medical degree or college education to take a quick glance around and see there are not enough people working. A kindergartner could assess the area and come to that conclusion without asking. You know it's short staffed and so do the employees. It's one of those things that doesn't need to be said, it is just understood. Plus you have now just put the employee in a bad spot. Of course they are going to lie and say there is enough staff, just too many patients. Then they are going to get mad because they just lied to cover for some managers at home collecting a big bonus for it being short staffed. It brings up in their

minds just how much they hate that those bastards won't hire extra help so it's not overcrowded with unsafe work conditions. They know they will never come into a shift when it is fully staffed and you just reminded them of this. Now they're frustrated with themselves because they lied to protect fake management and remember just how much they hate the staffing issues. Just save the trouble and don't ask. You can assume that 90% of the time you're in an emergency department it will be short staffed. And now, that employee is mad at the people who called out to make it even more of a staffing problem. More importantly, they are furious at themselves for not calling out.

42) Don't complain about the wait.

Well, to be quite honest and to the point, if you are well enough to keep coming up complaining about how long you've been waiting, you're well enough to go home. If whatever it is that you deemed to be an emergency is that bad you'll sit the fuck down, read those shitty waiting room magazines, and wait your turn. This is an emergency department you just walked into, unless you're practically dying, it's going to be a while. No matter how much you complain about the time, or who you complain to, nothing is going to make it shorter so you might as well quit wasting your breath. I know, it is a long wait, and I would probably be frustrated too.

Difference is I'm getting paid and have to be here. You aren't and you don't, so, bye.

43) Don't threaten to leave and go somewhere else.
This was always one of my favorite tactics, and will never work 100% of the time. I'm not sure if you noticed the other sixty motherfuckers breathing down my neck or not, but please, go on, threaten a staff member that you're about to get it down to fifty-nine motherfuckers bitching at me. Why are you even coming to me with these threats? The look on my face has to be telling you I could give a fuck whether you stay or go. Why are you standing here like I'm about to beg you to stay so you can bitch at me for another few hours? Do you need a fucking map to the exit, or some shit? It's been in the same location since you first got here. Look, this hospital isn't going out of business any time soon and I'm getting paid by the hour whether you stay or go. You leaving will affect my life and pay zero percent. So, uh, don't talk about it, be about it. You're just going to go start from scratch someplace else and chances are they're sending your ass right back here because they couldn't help you. Either shut the fuck up and wait your turn or walk out of that exit. No one is going to try to persuade you to stay and everyone is going to clock out at the same time with the same pay.

44) Don't tell me you hate this hospital.

Guess what, motherfucker? Me too. Mainly, because of bitches like you. You hate this hospital, the people here, and how you get treated. Yet here you are, in the place you hate, bitching about how much you hate it. What do you think I've been doing since I started getting ready for work? Bitching about how much I hate the hospital. I will continue to say it in my mind for my entire shift, then I will really get into how much I hate it, and you, on break with my buddies. The only difference is I am getting paid, while you are just wasting time and energy. I'm not sure if you noticed but I went completely blank, and blacked out as soon as you started saying how much you hate this place. Believe me pal, if a pissing match is what you came for I can out piss you on how much I hate this place and fucks like you. Leave. There's a big fucking sign that reads "exit" right over there. Generally speaking, if a person hates a place, they leave the first opportunity they get. They usually just walk out without publicly declaring how much they hate it. Then they usually will not go back to that place unless it is under new management or ownership or some shit like that. Same staff, management and doctors, same wait times and big crowds, nothing has changed. Please just proceed to the exit and shut the fuck up on your way. You hate it, I hate it, we all hate it. Let us just suffer together in silence, or go find a place you don't fucking hate.

45) Don't ask if you can come back later.

Sure you can. We're open all day every day. Doesn't mean shit is going to change. Chances are the same people will be laid up in these halls and in that waiting room when you come back later. By asking if you can come back later, you are actually stating you realized you are in fact NOT having an emergency and should go home. I encourage this. Go home and get some rest in the comfort of your own house. Chances are you're going to get some rest in your own bed and realize not only were you not having an emergency, but there is no need for you to come back. Take in your surroundings, do a self-evaluation of why you are there to begin with, and remember the place you are in is for emergencies. Then just take a moment to realize how fucking dumb that question is before you ask it. Just leave quietly. If you're in an emergency department and thinking you can come back later for your "emergency", you don't have a fucking emergency to begin with. Get the fuck out of here with that question. Your grade school teachers were wrong, there is such a thing as a dumb question, and this is another one of them.

46) Don't say everybody is just standing around doing nothing.

No shit. Before I really dive into why this is not a good path to go down, let me point out the obvious. In life, if you want help, you should not begin by telling the person you're asking that he or she is just standing around not doing shit anyway. That will almost 100% of the time get you nowhere. What do you think that is going to accomplish? Like a light is going to go off in my head and I'll think "you know what, he's right, I'm not doing shit, maybe I should help". Now to the next part of why you shouldn't say this; everything is in the open in a hospital. Employees work eight and twelve hour shifts. Of course there are people just standing around. I don't have to come to your job to know that you're not engaged in work every second of every minute of every hour, so let's just shut the fuck up on that fact alone. You have been assessed, medicated, put in for testing, and now you are waiting just like all the other motherfuckers in here. What else do you want me to do? Should I be doing push-ups or mopping the floor? You tell me, because I'm not sure what the fuck you want from me. Yeah, I'm standing around because my work is done. Let me be the employee and you be the fucking patient. If you think I'm going to run up and down the halls offering out hand and blow jobs until we have a room for you, you're wrong. It's an emergency department, and you're currently not dying so go sit the fuck down. I'm not here to fluff your fucking pillow, tuck you in and rub your head until you fall asleep.

47) Don't mumble while you walk by a staff member or they walk by you.

Asshole. If you want that as a label, by all means mumble, but either speak up or shut up if you do not. This is immediately what I think of you, because chances are it was an asshole thing that you mumbled. I could ask you what you just said but you will just cower and say nothing so why waste my breath. Just like you should not have wasted yours by mumbling. It's only about to play out in my favor if we engage in a battle of wits. You were afraid of this to begin with that's why your ass didn't speak up. I already have the upper hand because I used my words clearly to call you out and ask what the fuck you just said in a professional manner. Now that I think of it you're probably correct in just saying nothing because now I'm ready to go verbally ape shit on you. I'm going to thoroughly embarrass you in front of every person within ears reach. I'm going to do it professionally, sarcastically, clearly, loudly, and in a very demeaning manner. You just fucked up because I have been waiting for this moment all night and you just tossed out the bait. Well, I'll swallow that hook because you just reeled me into this verbal lashing that you are about to receive. I'll have you mumbling and stumbling, stuttering until I get to the point where I want you, which is dead silent, head down, contemplating why you decided to mumble that dumbass shit to begin with. Don't mumble. It will always end badly for you.

48) Don't act like a tough guy when being assaulted is what put you in the ED.

First off, you're standing there swollen and bruised, split open and bleeding. It's obvious you're no fighter by the evidence left all over your face from your first defeat of the night. You have no defense, obviously keep your guards low, and have poor reflexes. Judging by your coordination and reaction time, you are either under the influence of some intoxicating substance or have taken severe punishment to your head throughout your amateur street fighting career. I'm sober. I have been in this building smelling shit, vomit, piss, poor hygiene, failure and weakness for the past several hours. I have been listening to a hundred different people in every direction I turn, with a million different complaints. I'm angry. Now I have some dickhead who just got picked apart in a fight telling me I'm a pussy and talking shit on my family. Do you think I'm smiling because I'm entertained? Nope. I'm smiling because I can't wait for you to swing on me so I can put your record at 0-2 for the evening. And, guess what? All the other homies wearing scrubs are watching and cannot wait to jump in. Don't confuse those scrubs and educational degrees for weakness, it's only going to end in your demise. Save yourself some face and just stick with one loss for the night. You will get worn out twice in one night if this is your plan. Just suck up that loss and wait your turn quietly.

49) Don't say you know what to do because you are in school.

Oh, shit! Why didn't you say you were in your first semester of nursing school when you signed in? Hey! Hey, guys! Look! We have a nursing student that's a patient! See. Nobody gives a shit, so don't tell me how to do my job. I would love to chat it up about how great that is that you are in school, but I am sure by the look on my face you can tell I really don't give a fuck. I can see the innocence in your eyes, the care in your smile, and the difference you think you're going to make in your voice, but take a look around. No textbook is going to get you through this. You better toughen up and kill that spirit or these halls will eat you up. Come see me when your eyes are glazed over with numbness and your soul is calloused. You won't find that lesson on any page in your book, so save your school lessons for the classroom. I don't have the time, nor the shit to give about your studies in the middle of this chaos.

50) Don't come in for a pregnancy test.

What makes you fools think this is an emergency and can't wait until your local convenience store opens in the morning? Unless you plan on pounding a bottle of tequila and inhaling some nose beers this evening you can wait. This usually comes down to a money thing. Look, I'd rather have you come to the emergency department to ask me for money to buy a pregnancy test than sign in to get one. If you don't have the money to buy a pregnancy test you damn sure don't have the bread to cover this visit. I'm sure the hospital charges you at least three times the amount you would pay at a store. Then add up the price of being told the results by medical professionals instead of just looking at it yourself in the comfort of your own home. What would have cost you ten bucks at the local store has now just cost you a few hundred at the emergency department. Since you weren't willing to give up a Hamilton, you sure aren't going to pick up the tab for a few Benjamins. So, we might as well put that visit on the house's tab and make everybody there working pay for it in their taxes. Save yourself from pissing off everyone in the department, save yourself some money and time, and an endless supply of dirty looks. You should not be fucking raw anyway, if you cannot afford a pregnancy test you really cannot afford a kid.

How about we switch over to bodily functions? One would think you cannot really fuck up in situations where you have to puke, piss, or shit. I beg to differ…

51) Don't make yourself vomit.

You aren't fooling anyone. If you honestly think that with all the staff walking around nobody would see you, you are sadly mistaken. Not only did someone see you but they went and told everyone they know that you're gagging yourself down the hall to puke. Then a nurse is going to come talk to you with a very stern and loud voice. They don't have to be loud about it, but they want everyone in the surrounding area to know there's a bullshitter over here. Once they get done calling you out and embarrassing you in front of the other patients they're headed back to the computer. Yup. They're about to thoroughly document your shenanigans, so everybody you encounter for the rest of your visit knows you're a fucking faker. They're about to fuck you so hard with professional words on your chart, while they unprofessionally talk shit on you with their coworkers. This is chess, not checkers. You just jumped the board and made a costly mistake for a fast victory, while I sat back and played out the next ten moves in my head. Check mate, fella.

52) Don't vomit on the floor.

Hey buddy, like shit, sometimes, puke happens too. It's just unavoidable from time to time, and that's totally understandable, this doesn't apply to those instances. What I am talking about is you drunk and intentional offenders. Motherfucker, I just gave your drunk ass a basin to puke in since your weak ass can't handle your liquor. What do you do? Totally ignore the basin, put your head over the stretcher, and viciously vomit all over the floor. Now the entire triage area is polluted with this intoxicating fragrance of regurgitated noodles and fruity flavored vodka. Thanks, asshole. Then there is that attention seeking, pissed off patient that is fully coherent and capable of using the basin. Nah, fuck that though, right? Your punk ass would rather have people clean it up, and put on a show for the others waiting. If this was my house I'd snatch you off your stretcher by the hair and rub your face in the mess to teach you not to do that again. Unfortunately, I would catch numerous charges for that route. I'm just going to document so everyone you encounter for the rest of your visit will get a thorough description of how big of an asshole you are. It might seem petty, but I can't wait to get to my computer to poetically destroy your character on your medical record. Have fun cleaning up the mess I made for you to clean up, fucker.

53) Don't vomit on yourself.

That nice outfit you picked out for your big night is now ruined, because you didn't have the strength to move your head. That long hair you have is going to be crusted together with a terrible smell in the morning. All that time and effort you took in getting ready is now ruined. You were looking your best, feeling great about the night. Now you're laid up in an ED because you went too hard, and all that preparation you took is now painted with your own vomit. Puking all over yourself is a complete disaster all around. You're failing staff, your loved ones, surrounding patients and visitors, and most importantly you're failing yourself.

54) Don't piss on the floor.

It is really astounding how often this happens. What's even more astounding is the male to female ratio of pulling off this move. I have seen just as many females pop a squat in the middle of a crowded hallway as I have seen men whip their dick out and piss where they're standing. Usually there is some kind of mind altering substance on board. I understand drinking a lot makes you urinate a lot, but come on. For Christ's sake, try to have some common decency. You're not in the fucking club with a bunch of other drunk assholes. There is children and g-ma's all around. Nobody wants to see that. I am sure you can hold it for just a few moments until a bathroom is available. And if not, a sheet and a urinal provides at least some privacy and self-respect. They even make them for females these days. Let's try to stay at least half way classy.

55) Don't soil your pants.

Again, this doesn't apply to everyone, as some times it is just unavoidable. This one goes out to you drunk fucks, yet again, with soaking wet jeans, smelling like day old piss. Your ass is going to stay in them until you're sober enough to walk out of here because I'm not changing you. This also goes out to those fuckers who are so huge they don't even attempt to exert the energy to getting to a restroom. Nah, fuck that noise and hard ass work. You would rather just ring your bell and have a crew of motherfuckers roll you all around and clean you up. Fuck you. Every staff member in your room has malicious thoughts running through their mind while they hold and wipe you. Then when they leave they all exchange ideas of how they would really like to make you someone else's problem. Whether it is getting you admitted and out of the department or getting you moved to another area within the department. You can rest assured that the people caring for you are diligently working to get you the fuck out of their assignment in the quickest manner possible. Just don't do it if it's controllable. I don't care how much you make or how nice of a person you are, nobody enjoys cleaning up someone else's shit and piss.

Now we'll touch on basic accountability for yourself and children…

56) Don't blame me for not having shoes.
Look, I have rushed out of my front door a countless number of times. Not once, no matter what the reason was, did I forget to put on shoes. I have visited places all around the world, never have I lost track of where my shoes were. I've lost a lot of things in my life but never a pair of shoes I was walking in. If you can stand there as an adult and tell me I need to find your shoes you have quite a bit of growing up to do. Don't lose your fucking shoes and we won't have to play the blame game. Simple. I can assure you that no staff member gives a fuck whether or not you know where your shoes are. Chances are that a lot of them have small children who are responsible for their own shoes. They aren't going to worry about an adult incapable of this responsibility.

Speaking of shoes…

57) Don't bring your kids in without shoes on.
The only reason your kids should be with no shoes on is if they are being seen for two severed feet. In no way whatsoever is it cute to see a child running around in an emergency department with no shoes on. These floors are covered with bodily fluids and diseases. I don't even walk in my house with the shoes I wear in here. And, there you are, letting your kids raw-dog the fuck out of that filthy floor. The only time those floors get cleaned is when some asshole drives a Zamboni around pushing dirt around and blowing dust balls in the air. Jesus Christ. Just soak in all the shit that happens on those floors and you're letting your kid play on them like it's a fucking sandbox. You have shoes on, why would your child not? That's rhetorical, I really don't want to hear your bullshit reasoning for this situation that is unable to be justified in my opinion.

I'll take this moment to transition into a few tips for babies, since I just talked about young kids...

58) Don't act like a rectal temperature is a terrible act on your child.

It is the most accurate way to document a temperature on a baby. I'm not shoving a fucking broom handle up there, relax. You've had it done, I've had it done, we've all had it done to us multiple times. Believe me, I don't want to put this up there anymore than you want me to, so let's just get it over with. I don't need you coaching your baby through it like I have them strapped to some kind of torture device. It takes just a few seconds and is only a little bit of pressure. You act like I'm anally raping your baby with this thermometer probe. I wish I had some kind of magic wand to wave around and get a temperature, but I fucking don't. I don't get enjoyment out of hearing your baby cry and you acting like I'm doing something evil to them. Let's get this shit over with. Save the drama and hold this little motherfucker tightly, so I can get in and out. Goddamn, I hate parents like this.

59) Don't ask if you have to take the diaper off for a rectal temperature.

You do know what a rectal temperature is, correct? I'm about to lube up a thermometer probe and stick it inside of your child's rectum. You just stripped your kid down to the diaper and stopped. This isn't a game of darts and I don't have some diaper piercing probe. What the fuck? Of course I want you to take the fucking diaper off! I'm not going to guess where your baby's asshole is and try to hit it with a probe that I just blindly shoved through their diaper. I'm not sure what all brings your baby in today, but I can assure they'll be getting seen for a bruised up taint before they leave if that's how you expect us to get the temperature. Just take a moment to visualize those attempts at hitting it through the diaper. Now that you've taken a moment to think about it, if you still don't realize how fucking dumb of a question it is, then you shouldn't have any kids to begin with. Naked. Your baby needs to be naked from the waist down if you want to proceed. If not, I'll just document you refused it because you're too stupid to grasp the concept.

60) Don't just lay your baby down and watch the medical staff struggle.

Despite their size and looks some babies can be real bulls. It can be a struggle to get vitals at times. Parents can tell the staff member is struggling to keep your baby still and calm during this process, because you're standing there fucking watching them or on your goddamn phone. And if that's not enough, you should know how strong and wiggly your baby is from personal experience, because it's your fucking baby. This isn't child drop-off, and I'm not some miracle worker, nor a fucking baby whisperer. Get your ass over here and hold your baby while I do this shit. It's yours, you are allowed to touch it. It's not like I take over ownership because I was the last to touch your baby. Put down your phone and get up in this action. This isn't some kind of parent break room. I'll walk right out of that door until you're ready to start participating in your baby's care.

I think I'll break off from some triage and children action for a moment to swing focus onto the waiting room. Let's be honest, that place can be packed and get a little sporty. You are forced to sit in a room that reeks of both body odor and fluids. There's probably some bullshit channel stuck on the television that you don't like and who knows what's all over those magazines from last year sitting around. It can be miserable waiting out there, but that doesn't mean it should be free of *Don'ts*…

61) Don't be a waiting room heckler.

Every time I open the door to call a name you have some smartass remark or childish reaction to that fact that it wasn't yours called. I know you probably have a lot of questions about what is going on back there that is taking so long. Let me go ahead and answer them all for you. None of your fucking business. I'm sure you have a lot of questions about wait times and place in line. I'll answer all of those for you as well. I don't fucking know. Your wait time and place in line changes with the second hand on the clock. These things cannot be answered, and if someone does answer it, they are lying to you. So don't ask me every time I open up the door. I'm just going to say "give me a few minutes and I'll check", but I'm never going to check. Then when you ask me what happened I'm just going to say "I got tied up and forgot, give me a few more minutes". I'll play this game until you finally latch onto another employee. All that huffing and puffing you're doing while other names are called is just annoying the waiting room crowd. Trust me you don't want that crowd ganging up against you. This isn't a fucking game show, it's an emergency department, so act like it.

62) Don't ask to change the channel in the waiting room.

I swear it must be hospital policy to immediately throw away the remote control to the television. All the new ones I've seen go up in waiting rooms and

I've never seen a remote for any of them. I must be honest, I wouldn't change it if I did know how to. Mainly because it's not my priority, and I don't have to sit out there. So, by default, I don't give a shit what's on out there. Then there's the fact that nobody would agree on what to watch. I'm not standing out there, flipping through channels until we get a majority vote. Fuck that. No, nobody here knows how to change it or gives a shit about changing it, so don't ask.

63) Don't ask for coffee supplies in the waiting room.
I'm not a fucking barista and this isn't your local coffee shop. Drink what's out there, or don't drink it at all. If you think I'm going to run around looking for sugar and sweeteners, creams and milks, so you can whip up some kind of homemade soy latte out there you're wrong. Get out of my face with that shit. I'll come wipe down the coffee counter and sit out my tip jar, while I'm out there restocking sugar and shit. It's an emergency department, not a place you go to enjoy the free coffee. I'm already doing the job of three different job titles. I'm not willing to take on a fourth as the coffee person. Walk your ass to where they sell coffee if you want it to fit your taste preference perfectly.

64) Don't say the vending machine took your money.
Reading over your complaint here, I see you shouldn't have been at the fucking vending machine

to begin with. However, you were, and now you're out a couple bucks. Why are you even bringing this up? Do you think emergency departments keep change drawers by the lead nurse for these exact situations? They don't. If you brought it up because you think I'll spot you a couple dollars since I feel sorry for you. I won't, and I don't. You got beat for a dollar and a quarter, suck it up as a loss, and move on. Nobody gives a shit the vending machine took your money, and nobody is going to reimburse you for your waiting room losses.

65) Don't harass the other people out there waiting.
This is not an opportunity for you to begin panhandling for spare change and cigarettes. This is not the time to ask personal questions to complete strangers about their visit. People out there are sick or sad, but either way don't want to deal with your bullshit. Nobody needs that and if you push the envelope too far, you will get kicked off the property. It's a waiting room not a hustler's corner.

66) Don't block the waiting room entrance.
Just because your closest to the door doesn't mean shit. There is no need to stand right on the other side of the door. I will intentionally open it with force and then apologize for hitting you with it. The wheelchair tactic is a real dick move too. Let's just park right here so nobody can get through. I'll move your ass in the far back corner of the waiting room, then let you

struggle getting back to your spot on your own. Nobody has time for that game of let's block the entrance and be an asshole. And if you're standing right there to sneak in, guess what, I'm wise to that game too. If you think I'm not going to stand there until the door latches shut so you can't get sneak in, you're wrong.

OK, then. The waiting room can be a wild and demanding place. Let's switch our attention to chairs for a moment. You will generally find two types in your local emergency department; stationary chairs and wheelchairs...

67) Don't move any chairs.

That simple. Don't move the fucking chairs. They are put in specific places for specific reasons. Some are to get blood taken, some are to wait for testing, some are for vital signs, but all are for you not to fucking move them. You just can't bear to stand for a few minutes, so you take it upon yourself to start rearranging the department. You're here temporarily, this is my house, so don't move the furniture around. I don't come into your living room rearranging shit, so don't come into my emergency department and do it to my triage area.

68) Don't use a wheelchair for fun.

If you don't need it get the fuck out of it, because I'm sure there is at least a handful of people standing around that actually need it. You aren't at a wheelchair freestyle event. Nobody thinks you're cool doing 360s and wheelies. All you're doing is getting in the way with that dumb shit, at a hospital you don't need to be in, sitting in a wheelchair you shouldn't be in either. Cut it out before I have to scold you like a kindergartner getting yelled at for running with scissors.

Since we're on annoying shit, let's get back to the halls…

69) Don't stand in the way.

You see that big stretcher with all the equipment attached to the patient and a few staff members hauling ass down the hall. You're about to see that stretcher drive right up your ass if you don't move. If the pace, all the equipment, and multiple members pushing didn't give you the hint we are in a hurry, I'm not sure what will. I don't have time to stop momentum, because you want to lollygag around in the fucking halls. We have the right of way, and this is like an eighteen wheeler against a smart car. You're about to get pinned up against the wall, and probably rubbed pretty hard as we pass by you. Don't just stand in the way being an asshole. Seconds matter with real emergencies, unlike your bullshit one.

70) Don't lie down on the hall floors.

Grow up. This isn't a place to act like a child who is unable to even stand because you're so sick. You are an adult. I'll just wait until you're ready to stand up, because I'm not throwing my back out picking you up. Plus, this floor is dirty as a motherfucker! You have your open mouth and eyes just rolling around where people bleed, puke, piss and shit. I can't imagine what you're soaking up down there, but I'll wait. You probably need some antibiotics, or some shit, now after that tantrum.

71) Don't make friends with the people next to you in the halls.

I'm not talking about if you are enjoying a civil conversation with someone to pass the time. No, that is fine. I'm talking about you motherfuckers who try to get the person next to you all fired up to rally against staff. You talk about how long your wait has been, and how nobody cares about you here. Now you got the guy next to you, rallying behind your complaints and bitching about the same shit you've been crying about. I'm just going to professionally tell you both to shut the fuck up. I can go toe to toe with all you fucks in an argument. I'll leave you both breaking the no mumbling rule, mumbling shit about me to each other as I walk away. Numbers don't work for your needs, so you can try to gain as many supporters as you want. It won't change a thing.

72) Don't become a drunk therapist.

Look, you're here because you can't handle your drink. Just shut the fuck up and sleep it off. No patient wants your drunk ass asking them how they feel, or encouraging them that it will be alright. No staff member wants to talk to you about their family or personal life, so just quit asking them about it. All you're doing by prying in everyone's business is annoying the hell out of them. Staff just has to ignore it or ask you to be quiet. Patients and visitors don't. If you annoy them enough and overstay your conversation, you're liable to get knocked out. Once again, this isn't some club and some very sober and annoyed people won't hesitate to physically make you leave. Just mind your own business and get some sleep. Before you wind up getting a cat scan and stitches during your stay, because you just wouldn't leave people alone.

73) Don't do narcotics in the bathroom.
If you're in the bathroom of an emergency department, shooting or snorting something up, you really shouldn't be there to begin with. If you are there for rehab you obviously are not ready to commit to it. You are here now though, and if you're going that hard chances are that you're going to overdose in there. Nobody probably really even paid attention that you went in there to begin with. Is that really the way you want to die? Overdosed on drugs, laying on the floor in a hospital bathroom? Or, if you're lucky, someone will notice and open the door. Then your high is about to get totally fucked. Yup, you're about to get a little pick-me-up by the name of Narcan. That good high you just spent your money on is all gone now. Not only is your high gone, but now you're going to have somebody sitting with you watching every move you make. That's some prison shit, not hospital shit. Don't get high in the bathroom, just don't.

Since I just mentioned prison, let me touch on a few don'ts to help remind you that is not where you are. In the emergency department, a lot of nights, it can be a coin toss between a hospital and a prison. I can assure you it is in fact an ED, and these next few will help you distinguish differences between the two…

74) Don't light up a cigarette.

There's this gas called oxygen. In the emergency department a lot of people are hooked up to it. A lot of nozzles are on even though nothing is connected, meaning they're just expelling pure oxygen into the air. That shit is highly flammable. That could very well be the last cigarette you ever smoke. You'll blow the shit out of that building, and people will probably die. Don't be an asshole and risk other people's lives, so you can get a nicotine fix in. I don't even smoke but if you are going to light one up, at least invite me over to enjoy a last smoke with you before we blow up.

75) Don't ask me for a cigarette.

No, I don't have a smoke, and if I did I wouldn't give you one. We're not hanging out in the yard smoking and joking. You're at a hospital in the fucking emergency department. What kind of response do you think you're going to receive? Like I'm going to say, yes, I have a cigarette. Yeah, wait right here, I have to bang out this CPR real quick then I'll come outside with you. Just get out of my face with that question, especially when you're a patient and not just a visitor. This is triage not some fucking bodega you can head down to and buy looseys.

76) Don't ask for a phone call.

Sure, you can have a phone call. What makes you think you can't make a call? Oh, you don't have a phone and need to use mine, that's why you're asking. Fuck no, snake. There's a courtesy phone in the waiting room, get to dialing. If that doesn't work, I will turn this into prison like terms. I'll let you use a desk phone, and you get one call. If you don't reach anyone, you're just assed out. There isn't a chance in hell anyone is letting you use their personal cell phone, so definitely don't ask for that kind of call. Other than that, feel free to use your own or any courtesy phone at your leisure. You're not locked up, staff isn't monitoring your calls to pick up code talk to the outside world.

77) Don't say we can't keep you here.

That isn't necessarily true all the time. If you're under the influence of a substance, or a doctor writes an order saying you have to stay, you have no choice but to stay. Other than that, you're right and we know that. Guess what? Nobody wants to keep you here. Feel free to leave at any point of your stay. Nobody gives a fuck. As you can see by taking a look around it's pretty damn busy and I'm sure there are about fifty other patients who would love to take your spot. Nobody is really even going to notice you left, so there's no need to say we can't keep you here. Nobody has argued that since you entered the building. I know you're just trying to get attention so you get a room. It's not working, but if you need directions to the exit I'll be glad to provide them for you.

78) Don't ask if you can get some fresh air.
Ah, the oldest trick in the triage book. And, by fresh air you mean a cigarette, correct? I understand your wait has been long, and you'd probably like to have a smoke, if you are a smoker. Just don't talk to me in code like I'm your CO, or just taking me for a fool. Even if I was gullible enough to believe that, I would know as soon as you enter back into the building. I'm not sure where you're from but every place I've visited, not once did the fresh air smell like cigarette smoke and ash. Look, I don't care if you want to go smoke. Just don't take me for a fool and say you're getting air, say you're going to have a quick smoke. I won't lose as much respect for you if you just maintain that honesty.

79) Don't say you are going to call your lawyer.
We've just established you can smoke, just not inside. We told you we know that we cannot make you stay, and while you're here you can call anyone you would like. I'm not sure why you would need to call your lawyer, but by all means go ahead. If that is a scare tactic, it ain't working. If your lawyer is willing to press whatever case you think you may have, I give no fucks. This place you're in has a team of highly paid attorneys to represent them. I'm guessing your lawyer isn't the greatest since your information sheet usually says you're unemployed or in a minimum wage position. Maybe you get a discount for having them on standby 24/7, I'm not

sure. However, whether you get destroyed in court or settle outside, it will affect my life and pay 0%, so go ahead and call them.

Ok, so now that you know you're in a hospital and not a prison, I feel this is a good time to transition into explaining where else you're not - a fucking hotel…

80) Don't say you haven't eaten all day.

Hmm, now that you mention it, neither have I. This is not my problem, and nor should it be expected to be my problem. You're an adult, you should have eaten something today. I bet the vending machine took your last dollar too. Usually hospitals are surrounded by establishments to get food. Hell, most of them have their own cafeteria and restaurants inside the building. Yet here you are, grown, telling me that you have not eaten all day long. I think I'll just continue to stare at you blankly and say "OK" until you leave and decide to tell someone else who doesn't care. Look, I don't care if you only ate once earlier in the day or even since yesterday. Chances are, any staff member you encounter has also not eaten, and will not eat until they clock out. If you are looking for hunger sympathy I can assure you that you will not find it amongst any ED staff member.

81) Don't be picky about the food.

You just complained that you haven't eaten all day with dozens of restaurants in the surrounding area. Finally, I decide to cave and get you some food so you'll shut up. You don't eat or drink what I have to offer you for free of charge. Well, I guess you weren't that thirsty or hungry to begin with then. Let me go see what else our chef can whip you up real quick in the 4 star ED kitchen. Get the fuck out of here. If you haven't eaten all day you'll happily eat something free that will fill your belly. If you don't like what I'm serving up then that's just too fucking bad. I'm not a short order cook serving hotel guests. Walk your ass to a place that caters to your food order if it's that important to you. Otherwise, shovel this into your cum dumpster and enjoy in silence.

82) Don't ask for an ED combo meal before you leave.
This is when you ask for a sandwich and soda before you leave. No motherfucker, this is triage, not a hotel lobby. We're not serving up a continental breakfast before you go out site seeing. This is an emergency department, you were treated and discharged, you may be on your way now. You don't stop at the front to get a drink and sandwich to enjoy in the lobby before you leave. Where have you ever done that at any other type of establishment. Leave, just leave. This is a medical facility, not a hospitality facility.

83) Don't ask for a to-go bag.
This is just as bad if not worse than asking for a combo meal. You were treated, and received your discharge instructions. Probably got some prescriptions as well, but that just isn't enough for you. Nope. Now you'd like some bandages, antibiotic ointment, and tape. Those slipper socks, go ahead and toss some of those in there too. It's a little chilly outside let me get a blanket in there, toss another pair of socks in while you're at it. Maybe go ask the doctor if I can get another pill before I take off. That should do it, I'll be ready to be on my way

after that. Yeah, right. Get the fuck out of here. Sign this shit and leave. I'm not covering your fucking tab for shit I don't even get for free working here. Get innovative and figure out a way to smuggle it out of there just like all the employees do. I'm not going to risk my job for a stranger when I have to risk it for myself smuggling things in and out.

84) Don't ask for a warm blanket.

What? Can I get you a hot towel for your face as well? Here, I'll open this cabinet and pull you out one room temperature blanket. If that's not good enough I'll grab you another one. Two room temperature blankets equal one warm blanket. Unless you're pushing 90 years old or a small child you get no warm blanket. Simple as that. If you don't meet that criteria then we're all out of warm blankets. How do you even know there's a blanket warmer in the ED? I'm no detective, but if you know that, you've been here too many times before. I'm sure that nice person who gave you one last time didn't realize we don't have those here. I'll be sure to pass on to them that we don't have warm blankets, we just have fucking blankets.

85) Don't say you don't have a ride home.

OK, I guess you're walking home then. That ambulance you came in is a one way service. It is not your personal escort to and from the emergency department. I understand it sucks, and it will take you considerably longer to get home, but it can be done on foot. You not having a ride is not my problem, nor my concern. You're an adult, so figure it out. You were big enough to figure out how to get here, you'll be big enough to get back home. And if you don't get home, my conscience is still clear. Your failure to plan and prepare is not my pickle to now solve. Get to walking, buddy.

86) Don't ask me to get you a ride home.

Not just no, but fuck no on that one. All the technology today, and with all the public transportation avenues available, make no excuses for not being able to accomplish this on your own. I'm not going to run outside to hail you a cab, or pay for your Uber ride home. I have never gone any place as an adult and expected someone else to provide transportation for me to get back home. I suggest you either get to mashing numbers on a telephone, or get to pounding pavement with your feet on the walk home. If your insurance doesn't provide you with a ride, neither will I. Figure it out on your own, dick face.

87) Don't leave your trash behind.

You were either just given a free meal, or your friends and family came to visit with sacks full of fast food. Either way, during your little hospital picnic you nasty fucks left your trash and crumbs all over the tables and floor. There's a garbage can right next to your chair, but nah, fuck that, you'll just leave it for us to clean up. Where the fuck are you from, and who the fuck does that? Throw away your trash you fucking pigs. At least leave a few dollars on your stretcher when you leave, so I don't feel so cheap after saving your life and cleaning up after your pig family. We aren't room service, so don't fucking act like we are. It's really elementary. You have trash and we provided you with a trashcan, so go ahead and use it motherfucker.

88) Don't put your stickers all over the furniture and counters.

This goes for when you're hooked up to a monitor and shit like that. This isn't the fifth grade where you're putting gum under the desk. Don't be a dick. You're putting stickers all over desks and counters with your chest hair and shit on them. Grow up and throw them in the same fucking trashcan we provided for your picnic trash. Nobody enjoys scraping them off of wherever you felt fit to leave them. And I'm sure the next patient to use that sheet and blanket doesn't want to see your glue stains all over them.

Just because we now know medical staff are not in the hospitality business does not mean that some customs and courtesies should not be used during your visit in the ED…

89) Don't demand things.

Give me? Get me? Get out? Get in here? I think I sense a need for help and I want to provide it, but it's hard to be sure with the tone of your demands. What I need to be hearing are things like please, excuse me, do you mind, when you get a minute, shit like that. It's ok, I have a twelve hour shift to teach you manners. You'll either learn them, or you'll go without. No big deal to me either way.

90) Don't use profane language.

I know you're probably wondering how I can say that after sharing so many profane words and thoughts throughout this book. Well, the difference is, I just thought it while you actually said it. My dictionary in street language is just as thick as yours. Shit, I probably have words for you that you never even heard before. I can cuss with the best of them, but in this situation I am not able to. So, instead I'm going to verbally destroy you with sarcasm and big words you don't know the meaning of and I probably don't either. The key is to be fluid and confident. I may not be making any sense, but to you I will be, and it will sound great in my mind. The only time language like that works is in war and prison. We're not in either, so let's keep it cordial and leave the potty-mouth at home.

91) Don't yell out for help.

Show some common fucking decency. I'm willing to bet everything I have that if you just stand in any emergency department for five minutes you will hear some fool yell out "NURSE!". Don't do that. It's as annoying as somebody chewing with their mouth open. Chances are it's some type of bullshit you need anyway. Nurses are like moms. You can yell out nurse a million times, and they'll only here it once or twice when it counts. They're good at blocking annoying stuff out and picking up on things like silence or sincerity in a person's voice. Not only that, but show some respect for other patients around. It's ignorant and nobody wants to hear your whiny voice yelling down the hallway. And, that's why you have a call bell, so you don't have to yell out like a scared child in the middle of the night after they just woke up from a nightmare.

Since call bells came up…

92) Don't overuse your call bell.

A call bell is a luxury, not a right in the emergency department. You think we have time to answer those shits fast enough to comply with company policy? We can't; nor do we want to try to; nor do we give a fuck about call bell policy. I just left your fucking room, and it lights up again?! Get fucked! I don't have time for your bullshit red light, green light games. I have important shit to do, and you keep fucking up my flow by pressing that button every two minutes. I'm used to this shit, I was built for it, spent countless hours of perfecting the skill of blocking out noises. You press that button too many times and I'll let it ring for the next ten hours when I get to clock out. Day shift will be answering that 9 p.m. call bell if you keep fucking around with it. I'll have my manager answer it, then take an ass-chewing for not answering it myself, before I run to it every time you ring it. I guess you're wondering what to do if you shouldn't yell out or overuse your call bell. Figure it the fuck out and find a happy median, or I'll ignore your yells and bells all night long.

93) Don't walk away in the middle of directions you just asked for.

I could care less if you get to where you need to be or not. I know every square inch of this department and you approached me. I know where the fuck I'm going, you're the one that does not. I'm trying to give you help, but I guess I don't know shit since you're walking away as I talk. You'll hit a locked door or wrong room eventually, and realize you should have actually listened to the answer of your question. I could have given you detailed step numbers, times, landmarks and locations. You chose to walk away in the middle of my directions like an asshole, so I'll quit talking and go back to something else I don't care about.

94) Don't come around the corner like you didn't just receive directions.

I see the defeated look in your face because you were unable to navigate the department on your own. I know you're lost because you didn't fucking listen. I know I just tried to give you directions but you said, nah fuck you, I got this. I know you need me to give you fresh details on the path you need to take to arrive at your destination. I know this. You know you just fucked up. You know you're about to ask somebody to repeat themselves after you just disrespected them by walking away mid-sentence. You know you should apologize, right? You know if you don't I'm going to give you directions to a wild goose chase, right? Pay attention this time, and show some fucking respect. You might just get to where you need to be.

These next few are very important to follow and respect when first meeting any given staff member…

95) Don't thank Jesus.

I respect your faith, but I see me standing here, not Jesus. Thank me. I'm sure if Jesus was that worried, he wouldn't have made you wait ten hours to see a doctor. Jesus isn't pushing this stretcher or giving medications, I am. For fuck's sake if you're going to give him a shout, give me one too, because I've never seen Jesus pull a twelve hour overnight shift in here. I do and I'm here, toss a thanks my way too. I can quit helping you out and let Jesus take over from here. Just let me know when Jesus is done, and I'll come back with your discharge instructions. Looks like all you needed were thoughts and prayers to get you feeling better after all. I am not even sure why I got involved with your care when Jesus has been by your side this entire time.

96) Don't ask me if you are going to die.

I never know how to answer this. How the fuck should I know, I just told you I'm not Jesus. We're all going to die, act accordingly. Are you going to die during your visit? I can't promise that, but I damn sure hope you don't. Not on my watch anyway, because I'm going to have a shitload of paper work to fill out, and meetings to attend if you do. Do you feel like you're going to die? Think you can hold out until I leave this assignment? I mean shit, you're here for a sore throat, but I'll do my best not to let you die. You should probably talk to Jesus a little more thoroughly about that question, as I do not have the answers you seek. I really hope you don't fucking die before I switch assignments though.

97) Don't say it's about time when your name is called.

Weird, looking at my watch, I'm right on time calling your name. Sorry about your wait, but you're on my time, I'm not on yours. Don't confuse that shit. Every time I call your name, it's not about time, it's the right time. If I thought I needed to call it earlier I would have. There was no need to bump you in front of others, so your name was just called at the exact moment I wanted to call it. I'm sorry you have been inconvenienced with such a ridiculous wait time. I'm sorry you feel your name was not called on time. Actually, that's a lie. I don't give a fuck if you think it was the right or wrong time to call you. The important thing is, I called you. So either shut the fuck up and follow me, or get out of my way so I can call the next patient right on time.

98) Don't tell me I look familiar.

No, I don't. And I'm sure if we're familiar with each other I would recognize you. I do not. Let's skip the small talk, and just get to why you're here. It's not like we're about to become best friends, or some shit like that. If we don't know each other well enough to address each other by first name, then we don't know each other. We are not familiar and you don't need to pretend we are. Just get your vitals done and skip the bullshit. It doesn't matter if I look familiar to you or not. The important thing is if I think you look familiar. If you look familiar I either know you as friend or family, or a shit-bag I ran into here before. You probably made a mark in my memory, so I never forget how much of an asshole you are, so don't fucking worry if I look familiar, worry if you look familiar to me or not. This is my house, not yours, I don't care if I look familiar to you.

99) Don't tell me I took care of you last time.

I know. This goes back to that looking familiar shit. The time before last time and the time before that visit as well. I know who you are because you've pulled more shifts in here than I have the past few weeks. We both know you've been here too many times lately, so let's not try to make lighthearted remarks to make the situation a little less awkward. I don't care about last time, I'm focused on why you're wasting my time this visit. I want to get this visit right so I hopefully don't have to look at your pitiful face my next shift as well. I see hundreds of faces a day, so you should not expect us to bond since I briefly was involved in your care during your last visit.

100) Don't ask if a certain staff member is working.

Do you know how many crazy motherfuckers come through the emergency department? A lot! I have no idea who you are, you could be one of them. I don't care if I just got done talking to the person you're referencing, I'm telling you they aren't working right now. Then when I get a moment I'll go tell said staff member you were asking about them if they're interested in saying hello to you. You don't just come in throwing around random names like I'm just going to tell you where that person is. These halls are like the streets, there's no snitching on whereabouts to strangers, not from the halls. I don't care if you are their mother, they aren't here until I clear it with them. You don't ask to see staff by name, they'll come see you if they want to. No person in that department is going to give out information about a coworker if they don't know you. They'll see you're there in the computer system if they want to talk to you.

OK, so, we've gone over several things you don't do in the unwritten laws of all emergency departments. Believe me, there are probably thousands more of them as everyone has their own thoughts on what you don't do when they're interacting with you. I just thought I'd cover basic ones, that in my experience, I've found the majority of hospital workers can all agree on.

My intention is not to guide you in the direction of being a perfect patient or visitor during your visit in the ED. The intention with this book is just to help you not be a complete helpless and annoying asshole. If you study this and follow the unwritten *Don'ts* that I have provided you with, I promise every staff member you meet will try their best to make your stay as smooth as possible. Follow these and everyone will be a little less stressed and angered during your visit at any ED in the world. Well, at least where I'm from. I can't vouch for the world, so don't quote me on that shit.

I know, I know, you're probably thinking I shorted you one *Don't*. After all, the fucking title does say 101, and not 100. Relax fuckers, I'm not shorting you one. I'll leave you with the most important *Don't* of them all, so I can finally finish this fucking book, and give you whiny bitches your money's worth...

101) Don't fuck up.

The most important don't of them all, and also the easiest to abide by. You actually have to go out of your way to fuck up in an emergency department. It's so simple. Just be honest while using a civil tone, and stay clear of profanity. Treat staff with respect and you will receive it tenfold in return. Let people take care of you, and stay out of their way while they perform their craft. And if you see someone taking a breather, there's no reason to be ignorant about it and make a smartass remark. They're professionals, not robots, and believe it or not they're really fucking good at their job. All you have to do is shut up, mind your own business, and wait your fucking turn to have a decent visit. Easy shit.

To everyone who bought this book...

With your purchase of this book you have helped me come closer to achieving my ultimate dream with this writing game. That dream is to quit my job and never work for anyone else for the rest of my living days. I will retire early to a lake house in a secluded cove of the lake. It will have a huge dock with a boat house to park my fishing boat in. The house doesn't have to be anything special but the view will be spectacular and breathtaking. I will spend my days fishing and writing, while sipping on the finest bourbons throughout my carefree days.

If you tell all of your friends how awesome this book is, I can get even closer to my dream. Of course they will love reading this shit too, and then tell their friends about it as well. Then their friends will buy it and so on and so on. I figure you all can make it happen in just a few months.

I would imagine you are wondering why you would try to help me retire early to my dream house and boat, spending my days doing absolutely nothing. That's an easy one. I'm not a greedy motherfucker, and I'm a pretty simple man. I enjoy good whiskey and barbeque. Of course I am going to have some parties that legends are made of with plenty of both previously mentioned items there. And, if you bought this book, you're invited! I will get some big floats to toss out in the lake, and we'll have a bunch of fun games to play. I'll even get a diving board and a slide put on the dock with a kegerator out there just for these huge events. It will be an incredibly good time.

I'm just kidding, assholes. After reading this book do you really think I am the type of guy to invite a bunch of strange motherfuckers to come hang out at my new lake house? No fucking way, pal. If you didn't know me before the lake house, you won't know me after it. My one buddy, who did some time for selling coke, told me I should make it clear that I was just joking about having all you fuckers over for a cookout. He picked up a lot of knowledge about laws while he was locked up, so I trust his guidance on this. He's the closest thing I have to a lawyer and doesn't want to see me getting sued or some shit like that for false promises made about some party you were never invited to. He probably really doesn't know what the fuck he's talking about but it did sound like a good idea to clarify that. It was a joke, I don't care how many copies you buy, you're still not invited over.

Seriously though, thank you all so much for your support! May you all become fans of my writing and spread the word to help me grow. Plus the more people you tell the easier it will be for me to stay fueled up on good whiskey and keep cranking out writings like this one. Next up are some *Don'ts* for staff and management.

That's right, none of you assholes are safe…

Some Special Thanks

I cannot thank Ashley Delsignore and Courtney Turner enough for offering their assistance in making this project come to life. Two things I'm terrible at are mastering technology and using correct punctuation. When I told these two women I wanted to publish a book their eyes lit up with excitement. I could see they were just as, if not more, excited as I was to make this dream come true. If it wasn't for their contributions this book would have never happened. Their enthusiasm and eagerness to put in work on a cover and editing pushed me to work harder on perfecting my craft. I look forward to working with both ladies on future projects. With the help of those two there is nothing but glass ceilings to smashing our way to the top.

I also have to thank the man who really made this happen. I will never forget the time he pulled me to the side in those busy halls I just wrote about in this book. He asked me what I was doing there. He told me I had a gift and that I should pursue it. To this day I'm still not sure I have what he was talking about. He was the first person who ever told me I was a writer. We parted ways as co-workers but for some reason that conversation has always vividly stuck with me. I would think about what he said from time to time over the next few years and slowly started to believe him. Without that conversation I never would have thought about trying to grab people's attention with a pen and pad. Thank you, Greg Cooper, for being the first person to tell me I could be a great writer. I guess I started believing you and here we are now.

All the ladies and gentlemen that relentlessly attacked those halls by my side time and time again. Your twisted sense of humor and strong work ethic carried me through many a night in that chaos. There are way too many to name all of you but you know who you are. I met some of the best people I know while working under some of the worst conditions. Thank you all! I hope I don't disappoint any of you while telling our stories of those twelve hour overnight shifts.

93388068R00061

Made in the USA
Middletown, DE
13 October 2018